Blogger Dog, Brito!

Written by Denise Fenzi

Illustrated by Jerrica Coady-Farrell

6/21

First published in 2016 by:

Fenzi Dog Sports Academy Publishing

Copyright © 2016 Denise Fenzi

Designed by: Rebeccah Aube | www.pawsink.com
Paws & Ink! A Creative Blend of Dog Training & Graphic Design

Illustrations by: Jerrica Coady-Farrell
www.facebook.com/feorasart

ISBN NUMBER: 978-0-9887818-6-3

Blogger Dog, Brito!

 **Search** [   ]

Recent Posts

My Sites

www.fenzibloggerdogs.com
www.denisefenzipetdogs.com

1

Welcome!

Posted by CaBrito

Welcome to my blog! I've been thinking about starting one for a while. It seems that everyone is writing a blog these days, and since I'm a modern kind of dog, I like to live a modern kind of life.

If you're not sure what a blog is, it's really pretty simple. It's a website on the internet where the writer can write stuff that comes into their head. The writer is called a "blogger," and whatever they write is called a "post." Anyone in the world can read the blog, and the best part is that the readers can make comments. Those show up at the end of the post! If you really like someone's blog, you can subscribe to it so you'll get emails telling you when a new blog is posted.

Having my own blog will give me something to do when Mom is too busy to pay attention to me. My mom has a blog, and she writes all the time. Now I will too! That's the plan, anyway; sometimes my attention span is short, and I get distracted from my best ideas. Mom says it's the terrier in me.

Unlike some dogs you might meet in blogs, I'm a real dog, and my stories are real stories! I have lots of ideas and feelings in my head. Sometimes I'm mad or sad, but most of the time I'm pretty happy with my life.

Hey, that reminds me- you don't know who I am yet! Well, my name is Brito. That's short for Cabrito. If you speak any Spanish, you know that Cabrito means "little goat." I was called Cabrito because, when I was extra small, I liked to jump and climb all over things, and also because I'm white and very scruffy, so I reminded people of a goat. But Cabrito took a long time to say, so now I'm just called Brito.

I'm no particular breed of dog, but people like to guess about what I might be. Mom calls me a terrier mix. That works for me since terriers are the brave and independent explorers of the dog world!

Now that I'm a grown-up dog (I'm two years old now!), I don't climb on things as much as I used to, but I do like to sit on Mom's desk while she writes. I've been told that dogs shouldn't sit on the desk, but I've seen cats that are bigger than me sitting on the desk, so why not me? And at nine pounds, about the size of a jug of milk, I don't think I'm big enough to break anything.

Well, except there was that one time my mom's glass fell over and landed on her computer, but I don't think that was really my fault. You see, Mom is left-handed, so the drink is always on the LEFT side of her keyboard. How was I supposed to know that she moved it to the RIGHT side? And when I hopped up on her desk, all happy and wiggly, how could I know that I would land on top of that overly full glass?

And that maybe, possibly, the drink in that overly full glass might somehow fall inside her computer? So you see, I would argue that the drink incident was a simple misunderstanding.

When I moved into my home, my mom talked to me a lot; soon I knew how to do a lot of things, much more than most dogs. That's because my mom is a dog trainer, and people from all over the world know of her through her writing, blog, and teaching. And because people know my mom, they know me. So I'm famous too!

I like being famous. Once, a total stranger came over to meet me when I was at dog training school. She said, "Hey, is that Brito?!" and walked right over to admire me. She didn't even say hello to Mom first! That seemed fair enough to me. Imagine if you met Clifford the Big Red Dog and Emily. Who would you say hello to first? That's right— Clifford! That's how famous I am these days, but my life sure didn't start out like that.

I'm proud of my mom because she's a very special person. But, as you will soon learn, I'm also a very special dog, so I think Mom and I were made for each other. I mean, really, how many dogs have enough going on in their lives to start their own blog? Mom and I have a lot in common. In particular, we're both storytellers at heart, so I'd say that I'm in my perfect home.

That reminds me, you don't know how I came to live here, so that will be my next blog! This story is not funny, but not all of life is funny, and I want to keep it real here. Don't worry, the story has a happy ending, so keep reading!

COMMENTS:

Theo (Great Dane) | Palo Alto, CA, USA
Brito! So great to see you online! You're going to raise the roof as a blogger! All the cool dogs have blogs! Can't wait to hear your stories!

Keegan (Collie) | Dartmouth, NS, CAN
Brito, now you're a writer, just like your mom! Welcome to blogging!

Champ (Terrier) | Portsmouth, NH, USA
OMG! I have similar problems with breaking overly full glasses and plates with food on them! I helpfully clean up the messes. They're delicious!

2

Brito Needs a Home!

Posted by CaBrito

When I was first born, no one knew how special I was. To be honest, I didn't even know how special I was, because no one wanted to keep me. I kept getting moved from one home to another. I don't know why I had a lot of homes, because I am not a bad dog. Yeah, I made some mistakes here and there, but who doesn't?

In my first home, I didn't know where the bathroom was, so sometimes I would pee or poop in the wrong place. Then I would get yelled at, which would scare me, so I started to hide when I had to go to the bathroom. The next thing I knew, they didn't want me anymore, and they gave me to a new family. Fine with me; I didn't want them either!

In my second home, there was a very big dog with very big feet. His big paws would step on me, and I would yelp and run away to hide. I hid behind the bed because he was too big to follow me there. Sometimes, big hands would reach in and try to make me come out. That was also scary, so I would growl. I didn't growl because I was mean; I growled because I was scared and I didn't know what else to do. It's not that I'm a scaredy cat or anything, but hey, I was just a puppy. Give me a break! I was trying to say, "Leave me alone!" but most of the time no one listened. In that house, they didn't understand dog language.

At first, I just stayed hidden behind the bed, but that was boring. So I started looking for something to do back there, and I found things to chew. Mostly it was trash that had fallen behind the couch, but sometimes I chewed up things that made my new family really angry, like wires or important papers. I also liked to chew because I was getting new teeth and my mouth hurt.

Anyway, I would hide behind the couch and chew things and growl when I got scared. And then that family didn't want me anymore, either. Even though I wasn't very happy there, I was starting to wonder if a not-very-good home was better than no home at all!

Next, I found myself in a place called a foster home where I had a foster mom. This lady didn't scare me. She didn't grab me or yell at me, and the other dogs weren't allowed to chase me around, so I didn't need to hide.

This lady liked me and taught me to be a good dog. I learned where the bathroom was, and that I should chew my toys instead of things that weren't mine, and even when I chewed the wrong things or got into trouble, no one got really angry about it. Hey, sometimes puppies make bad decisions! I wanted to stay in this home forever, but even though I was very small and filled with personality, there was really no room for me there, either.

Sometimes I pretend to be okay on the outside even when I'm sad on the inside, so maybe I looked like a happy dog to most people, but honestly, I was beginning to feel pretty bad about myself. There had to be someone looking for a small, white, scruffy dog who sometimes got into a little bit of trouble. I wanted to have a family to call my own, and it wasn't looking too good.

But then the dog trainer lady showed up. I'll tell that story in my next post, so be sure to check back soon!

COMMENTS:

Bruno (Lab) | Naples, FL, USA
This sure brings back memories— I had a lot of homes when I was little too! I was so scared when I sat in a kennel by myself and dogs were barking all around me. But then I got adopted by a wonderful family! I can't wait to read what happens next, Brito! Best of luck, and I'm going to subscribe right now!

Trish (Sheltie) I London, ENG, UK

Wow, your life sounds a lot like mine! I used to get scared when I saw big dogs, so I yelled at them to stay away. Then Mom started giving me treats whenever big dogs were near. Now I'm not so scared when the big dogs come around because I know that treats will follow... but I still don't want them too close. I'm sure glad I don't have to live with big dogs!

Sally (Border Collie) I Bar Harbor, ME, USA

I'm glad I've only had one home!

3

Brito Finds His Forever Home

Posted by CaBrito

One day, a lady came to help my foster mom train dogs. This lady likes dogs so much that she trains them all day long! I had never heard of that job before.

I watched her quietly and thought that she was really nice! I liked how she gave all of the dogs treats and taught their owners how to play with toys. I could tell that she was listening when the dogs talked to her and that she was teaching the owners to listen as well.

I wanted to talk to her, too! At the end of the day, after most of the other people and dogs went home, I saw my chance. While she was talking to the other humans, I brought her a toy. Sometimes humans are very slow about dog language, so to help her understand, I put the ball on the ground right in front of her feet where she couldn't miss it. Then I looked right up at her face, smiled a big smile, and wagged my tail.

Well, this human wasn't slow at all! She understood right away, and she threw my ball! She played with the other dogs too, but I could tell that she liked me the best by the way she responded every time I smiled at her. Wow, she was really paying attention to me! I liked the way I felt when she was in the room, so of course that made me want to spend even more time with her!

Then I heard the humans talking about me. I felt bad about what they said, but I pretended not to care. They told the dog trainer lady that I had already had a lot of homes. I worried that she might think I was a bad dog because of all of those homes. It sure didn't sound very good when they told my story! Maybe she wouldn't understand about the hiding and the peeing and the growling and how no one wanted me. I started to worry that she might not like me so much after all.

But this lady? She was smart! She said what I really needed was a permanent home! Next thing I knew, all of the other humans and dogs left the room. The lady sat on the floor with me. We played with toys. We ate a snack together. She held me on her lap and clapped and laughed when I smiled at her. I didn't want her to leave!

When the other humans came back in the room, they took me away, and the nice lady stayed behind. I could hear her talking on the phone, and I was pretty sure she was talking about me.

The other humans were being very quiet. They were listening, too. Yes, she was talking about me. I got worried because the conversation went on for a very long time. It seemed that maybe the person on the phone did not want another dog. That there might not be any room for one more dog, even a small one like me. It was touch and go for a while, I can tell you that for sure! I was so afraid to get my hopes up, but I really wanted this lady to take me with her!

Next thing I knew, the lady picked me up, put me in a special little box made just for dogs, and said I was going to live with her. Forever.

I didn't want her to change her mind, so I was on my best behavior. The lady took me on an airplane, and I stayed totally quiet. I figured I could introduce her to my full personality when we knew each other a little better.

When we arrived at my new home, I met more

people: my human dad, two boys named Nick and Chris (who would be my human brothers), and two dogs who would be my siblings. Their names are Lyra and Raika. I liked the boys right away, but the dogs... the dogs were big. I'd been in that situation before, and I was scared. But my new mom didn't let them chase me, and soon I knew that they wouldn't hurt me. In fact, I really like Lyra now! But Raika? Well, maybe not so much. She's kind of grumpy.

Anyway, I didn't need to hide behind the couch because no one was allowed to grab me, not people or dogs. And when I got scared, my mom would stand right next to me and pet me quietly. I felt so safe that I didn't need to yell very much anymore.

I didn't need to pee in the house because I was taken to the yard a lot, and I got lots of pets and attention when I peed outside. When I had potty accidents in the house, no one said anything; they just cleaned up and took me out to potty more often. It's not like I wanted to potty on the floor! But sometimes I would get so busy with what I was doing that I just stopped paying attention and an accident would happen. The whole family took turns taking me out to pee and poop so I could learn good potty habits.

My new family told me every day that I was wonderful. One of a kind! They spent so much time helping me be right that I never had any time to be wrong! That made me feel proud, and that's when I knew for sure that I really was a special dog.

When I first arrived at my new home, I didn't want to get my hopes up. A lot of people had told me that they would keep me, and then they changed their minds. But soon I knew that things were different here. It didn't take long for me to know that I would be in this home forever.

My mom likes to tell me how lucky she is to have me, and now I know that she was smart to take me home. It just took a while for the right person to come along and realize how much they needed a small, scruffy white dog in their lives!

I'll admit that I'm not the perfect dog, but hey, who's perfect? Some days I bark too much at the squirrels outside, and other times I yell at new dogs in public. I really don't like strangers picking me up, and I get jealous when someone else is getting something I want. But my whole family still loves me. My mom says there are no perfect dogs, and anyway, she isn't always so perfect herself. But that's a story for another day!

See, I told you that my story started out sad but ended up happy. Those are the best kinds of stories of all!

COMMENTS:

Bruno (Lab) | Naples, FL, USA
Brito, your story was a real nail biter! I was scared that the dog trainer lady might not take you home. Congratulations on your adoption! I hope she got lots of balls for you to play with. Tell her to stock up!

Champ (Terrier) | Portsmouth, NH, USA
I chase squirrels too! But I've never caught one.

Brito: Me either, but I practice a lot. Mom says that practice makes perfect, so I figure it's only a matter of time. Don't give up hope!

Lexi (German Shepherd) | Stowe, VT, USA

I get yelled at a lot when I make mistakes. You're a lucky dog, Brito!

Paula (Foster Mom) | Dallas, TX, USA

Brito! It's Paula, your foster mom! Wow, I'm so happy to see you online! I talk to your mom all the time on Facebook, so I've been watching your videos. I know that she loves you very much. Congratulations on your new blog. Great idea!

Brito: Hi Paula! I'm so excited that you're here. I still love you and appreciate all that you did for me. Don't forget to subscribe!

4
My New Family

Posted by CaBrito

I want to tell you more about my family. I've already told you about Mom. Now I will introduce you to the others.

Nick is my oldest human brother. He didn't say too much when we first met, just that I seemed to be very small and scruffy. I didn't know if he thought it was good to be small and scruffy or not. Nick is a teenager. Mom says that teenagers don't talk much, so I don't take it personally when he doesn't talk to me. Mostly he reads books and thinks about things and plays video games. Oh, and sleeps in late in the morning and complains about having to get up for school.

Nick is awesome when he sits on the couch and

works on his computer. I snuggle up nice and close so that I'm warm and comfortable. He doesn't seem to mind me being there. Sometimes he even shares his blanket so I'm pretty sure he likes me.

And now that I've been here awhile, I know that he is very good at opening the door and letting me out when I ask, even if I ask fifty times in a day. So he's a very good addition to my new family. Every dog needs a good door opener.

Then I met Chris. Chris is different than Nick. Chris talks a lot! He is always talking and drawing and playing with things and moving. With all of that talking, I don't think Chris is a teenager yet.

Chris loved me right away. He wanted me to sleep on his bed from the very first night, but Mom reminded him that I still had to learn where to use the bathroom, so I needed to stay sleeping in my little box. That made me sad since Chris has a great big bed and I was looking forward to sleeping there. And anyway, I was pretty sure that Chris would like my company at night.

I love Chris a lot. He likes to talk to me and draw pictures of me. But I do not like it when he tries to dress me up in silly Halloween costumes or when he wants to put me in the back of a toy dump truck and drive me around the yard. Mom has to keep an eye on him.

I met Dad next. I'm pretty sure he was the one that Mom talked to on the phone who didn't really want another dog. When I first arrived, I heard him say things like, "Don't we have enough dogs?" and "He

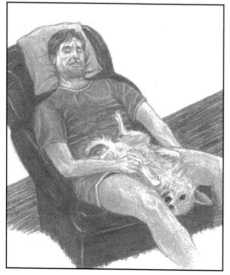

sure has a loud bark for such a little dog." Dad also says that I "don't have very much sense." That one concerns me a little since he often says it when I've done something I wasn't supposed to do, like slip through a hole in the fence that no one but me even knew about. I prefer to think of myself as an explorer with a healthy dose of curiosity than a dog who doesn't have much sense!

Fortunately for me, it appears that Mom cared more about keeping me than Dad did about finding me a new home, so… I got to stay. And anyway, I think I've grown on Dad. He talks to me in a squeaky voice, and he fixed all of the holes in the fence so that I can't escape and get hurt. He also has the perfect sized lap for lying upside down while I get a first class belly rub. That's how I know that he really loves me too.

And of course, there are the other dogs, Lyra and Raika.

Lyra is my best friend. When I first met her, I growled and backed away because that's what I do when I'm scared. And you know what she did? She lay down on the floor and put her head flat on the ground! Her tail was gently wagging at me, and I could see that she was trying to be small, just like me. In dog language, she was saying, "Let's be friends!"

Lyra and I play all the time. When I first arrived, Lyra would always lie down flat or even roll over so we could wrestle. I would climb on top of her and pretend that I knocked her over. But when I stopped being worried about her hurting me, we started to play games of chase, too.

Sometimes she forgets to be gentle, and I have to yell at her to be more careful. She feels bad when that happens, so she lies down again to show me that it was an accident and that she is sorry. I love Lyra.

Raika is my other doggy sister. She is not my friend. Maybe I shouldn't tell you this, but I don't like her very much, even though Mom says I love her "deep down inside." It's not like I want anything bad to happen to her; it's just that she's not much fun.

Raika is very grumpy. Whenever I ask Raika if she wants to play, she just… stares… at me. A few times, she has shown me her teeth when I was trying extra hard to get her to play. I know what that means in dog language— "stay away!" I'm pretty sure Raika would not hurt me; but hey, I understand when someone doesn't want to be my friend, and that's fine with me. The house is big enough for all of us, so I leave her alone most of the time.

Mom says Raika doesn't like dogs very much, and boy, is that true. Raika mostly likes Mom. A lot. She likes Mom so much that all she does during the day is follow Mom around and stare at her. It's ridiculous, if you ask me. I don't think Raika has ever had a thought that Mom didn't put in her head.

Pitiful. Mom says she is a herding dog, so she likes to cooperate with people. If you want my opinion, she's more like a sheep. Baa!

It's not that Raika is bad or anything. It's just that I think she could have more fun in life if she would get into trouble once in a while. Raika could be more like me and Lyra. I think Raika should try digging in the yard or chasing lizards or barking at the squirrels in the trees. Sometimes I can't help myself, and I tease her. I call her the "Fun police." Then Mom takes me out of the room and puts me on a time out. I don't like time outs, so I try to stay away from her most of the time.

Mom loves Raika very much, even if I can't figure out why. Mom says Raika is getting old and sometimes her body hurts, so she wants to be left alone. So we all live together, and I try to get along with her as best I can.

But I still don't think I like her.

So now you know my family! I love all of them, except maybe Raika, but Mom is really the most special. Maybe that is because she spends a lot of time with me and she is always watching to make sure that I am being treated right. She also listens to me to make sure that I am happy.

If you're thinking that Mom and I talk using regular words, that's not what I mean. Instead, I talk with my body, and I watch her pretty carefully, too. It's not hard for a dog to talk— we do it all the time with each other. The hard part for people is learning to listen.

Just like all dogs, I have been talking since I was a very young puppy, but sometimes dogs stop talking to people because no one is listening. My mom listens when I talk, so I have plenty to say. My mom is an expert dog listener. That means she is very good at dog language. But anyone can learn dog language; you just have to pay attention when your dog is talking!

In my next blog, I'll tell you a little about how Mom teaches me human words and how I can talk right back! Thanks for reading, and don't forget to subscribe!

COMMENTS:

Bruno (Lab) | Naples, FL, USA
Your human family sounds like mine, except that I have a teenaged sister instead of a brother. She is always texting her friends on her phone, and she rolls her eyes a lot. Mom says that is normal. I think she would benefit from more fresh air and a run in the woods, or maybe even a good roll in a cow patty!

Sally (Border Collie) | Bar Harbor, ME, USA
I don't think you are very nice about Raika. She sounds like a very good and well-behaved dog. Is Raika famous too? Her name rings a bell. Anyway, I think you should listen to Raika. She could teach you things.

Champ (Terrier) | Portsmouth, NH, USA
OMG Brito! You and I are so alike! I like to chase squirrels and bark and dig too! I dig so much that my mom made me a sandbox

and then buried my toys. I love it!
Now I dig in my sandbox instead
of in the flower garden. I think my
mom is much happier about that.

 Champ: PS Terriers are the best!

 Sally: That's totally uncalled for. If it weren't for us herding dogs, there would be chaos in the world.

 Champ: If it weren't for us terriers, we'd be overrun with vermin! Terriers rule, herders drool!

 **Pappy** (Pomeranian) | Joplin, MO, USA
Brito, I can totally relate because I have a sister that I play with all the time and a brother who is a useless little tattle tale.

5

Dog-Human Language

Posted by CaBrito

While it's true that my mom knows a lot of my dog language, she wanted me to learn some of her human words, too. For example, Mom wanted to teach me the word "treat." So in a happy voice, Mom would ask me, "Do you want a treat?"

Well, of course I wanted a treat, so most of the time I would say yes! I say "yes!" by wagging my tail, perking up my ears, and coming right to Mom with my happy face. Sometimes I wag my tail so hard that my whole body wags!

Every day, Mom would ask me if I wanted a treat, and I would wag my whole body, perk up my ears, jump around with my happy face, and say, "YES!"

Mom taught me the toy word, too. She would hold out a toy and ask, "Do you want a toy?" Then she would offer it to me! Who doesn't want a toy? So I would wag my tail, perk up my ears, and come over to take it as fast as I could! Now, if I want Mom to throw the toy, I use my dog language with her. I put the ball in front of her toes, back up, and smile at her face. She knows that means she should pick it up and play with me.

I know this might sound strange, but some days I just want to be left alone. I don't want to play with toys or snuggle with Mom. Sometimes I don't even want to play with Lyra. On those days, I will say "NO," when Mom asks if I want to play.

Do you want to know how I say "NO"?

If I don't want to play, my tail won't wag very hard when Mom talks to me, and my ears won't perk up. On a really bad day, I might even walk away or turn my head away or even give a little growl. Mom says that's okay because it's the only way that I can communicate. After all, I can't talk like a human can! It just means I don't want to play. I want to be left alone.

See how Mom and I have real conversations? It's not all about her; it's about me too! My mom loves me enough to take the time to know me and to listen to what I want. It makes me kind of sad when I think about my first homes where no one made any effort to talk to me. I was so lonely!

Next time I write, I want to tell you about one day when I went out with my mom and met some new people. And because Mom knows when I'm saying yes and when I'm saying no, I even made new friends! So make sure you subscribe to my blog to get regular updates every time I post!

COMMENTS:

Lexi (German Shepherd) | Stowe, VT, USA
You are so lucky that your mom listens to you! In my house, no one listens to dog language. Mostly I am left outside by myself.

Brito: Wow, Lexi. I'm sorry to hear that! Try barking or howling all night and see if that makes them bring you in. It worked for a friend of mine when the neighbors started to complain about the noise. - Brito

Bruno (Lab)| Naples, FL, USA
My family plays with me, too, and I learned the "ball" word right away! We go to the park every day and play ball. Chasing a ball is the best! Or maybe eating is the best. No. Chasing a ball! No. Eating! I can't decide! I love balls and eating!

Sally (Border Collie) I Bar Harbor, ME, USA
You jump up and down when you want something? I just wait politely for my mom to notice me. Must be the terrier in you. They are so impulsive.

6
Making New Friends

Posted by CaBrito

One day, Mom took me to a park. She brought my toys and my treats so that we could play together. First, I walked around and sniffed the plants, and the trees, and the grass, and almost everything! There are so many smells in the world, sometimes I can't even believe all the things there are for me to know about. And being a curious dog, I really like to explore! Not much gets past me, let me tell you!

My mom tries to be patient and lets me walk around exploring. Sometimes I think she would like to do other things, but hey, that's what a relationship is all about! Give and take, right? Sometimes we do what I want, and sometimes we do what she wants. For example, sometimes my mom wants to get exercise, so then we walk really fast and I don't get to stop and smell things. Other times we stroll along, and I get to smell just about everything.

When I get tired of smelling things, we play. We run back and forth on the grass playing chase, or Mom throws my ball and I try to remember to bring it back, but sometimes I forget and just chew on it. That's fun too! When it's a really warm day, we lie in the sun and I get a belly rub.

Wait a sec— I'm getting away from my story! I wanted to tell you about making friends!

One day, Mom took me to the park, and it all started out like usual. Then a whole bunch of schoolkids came to the park; they were being very noisy! Some of the kids were afraid of dogs, so they stayed away, but others came running over full speed, right at me!

I guess Mom saw this coming because she stepped in front of me, and before they could swarm me, she had all of the children sit on the ground. I'm glad she did that, because I was a little worried about all those kids! Then the kids asked if they could pet me, and do you know what Mom said? She said they had to ask me first.

Wow! I've never heard that rule before, but it's a pretty good one. It's my choice! To say "yes," I would walk right up to them with a wagging tail. To say "no," I would stay away. The kids sat on the ground, patted their laps, and called, "Brito, do you want me to pet you?" And there they were, all sitting and calling to me.

Well, let me tell you, I was in heaven! I love little kids! At first, I was overwhelmed because so many were calling at once and I didn't really know where to start. But then I sat on their laps and kissed their faces. I wiggled my body and wagged my tail and showed my happy, smiling face so they would know how much I liked them.

Sometimes the children would try and stand up and walk towards me, but Mom would remind them of the rules, and they would sit back down and wait for me to go to them. I really appreciated that Mom was looking out for me. I like kids, but when they scare me? Then not so much.

The hardest part for the kids was waiting their turns. I understand that, because I'm not always good at waiting my turn either. Just ask Raika. Any time I try and cut in line, she's right there to tattle on me. That's why I call her the "Fun Police" when Mom can't hear me.

After a while, most of the kids left to play on the play ground. Two little girls stayed with me. One of them scratched my back and talked nicely to me while I sat on her lap. It was so nice, being in the warm sunshine with my new friends.

Suddenly, something changed. The girl who wasn't petting me got jealous because she wanted to pet me, too. She forgot the rule and reached over and tried to pick me up without asking me first! I wasn't looking at her when it happened, so I got really scared when she grabbed me! Can you imagine if a person you did not know just reached right over and tried to scoop you off the ground? Let me tell you— it was terrifying!

Just then, Mom saw what was happening, and she got on the ball. She stepped right in and took me back! Boy was I grateful! I was feeling so scared that I almost growled at the girl to make her put me down! People don't like to be growled at.

I kind of wanted Mom to yell at the girl, but she didn't. She just reminded her to sit quietly and to always ask the dog if they want to visit.   We tried again, and this time was much better! The little girl sat on the ground and asked me to come over by patting her lap and clapping her hands. I had to think about it because I was still worried, but then I decided that I wanted to see her just as much as she wanted to see me, so I went over and wagged my tail and put my ears up.

And then she scratched my back and my chest just the way I like, and when I rolled over, she even scratched my tummy! So I guess it's a good idea to give kids second chances, because it worked out for both of us!

After a while, I was tired of playing with the girls, and I walked away. They were listening to my dog language, and they let me go without chasing me. What started out a bit scary turned into a great day!

Speaking of being jealous, I remember a day when I was jealous of Raika and Lyra, just like the little girl who was jealous at the park. "Jealous" means I was mad and sad all at the same time. But you'll have to wait until my next post to hear that story since it's time for me to help Dad in the kitchen. He's about to get dinner ready for the family, and my job is to pick up any food that falls to the floor. It's a fun job! I'll be writing again soon, so don't forget to subscribe!

COMMENTS:

Bruno (Lab) | Naples, FL, USA
My favorite kids eat ice cream cones. Sometimes I nudge their hands very gently so the ice cream part falls to the ground. I eat whatever hits the floor because I have that cleaning up job too! Ice cream cones are the best.

Brito: I'll have to try that hand nudging thing; thanks for the tip!

Theo (Great Dane) | Palo Alto, CA, USA
I like kids, too, but sometimes I drool on them when I see their ice cream cones, and then they look disgusted and run away.

Sally (Border Collie) | Bar Harbor, ME, USA
I don't like it when kids pet me because they have sticky fingers. I always say no when they ask. Also, you should always bring the ball back when your mom throws it. That is how the game is supposed to be played. That's why it is called "fetch" and not "keep."

Champ: Sally, do you ever have fun in life?

Sally: Yes, I'm simply more mature than you, so I have different hobbies.

Champ: "Mature" sounds like a lot of "manure."

Pappy (Pomeranian) | Joplin, MO, USA
Sometimes I get jealous of my siblings, too, so I can't wait to hear your next story!

Stella (Lab) | Ottawa, ON, CAN

Hi, Brito. I've never commented on a blog before, but I think your mom's rule is the best rule ever! In my house, the kids lie on top of me! I use my best doggy language to ask them to stop, but they don't listen.

Brito: Hi, Stella. Wow, I'm really sorry to hear your story. My advice is just try to hide under furniture where they can't get to you. Good luck, and let us know how it goes.

Stella: Hi, Brito. Thanks for your advice. I wish I had my own space where the kids were not allowed to go. Thanks again!

Brito: Good luck, Stella. I wish more humans would learn dog language.

7
The Best Toy!

I told you I would share my jealousy story, but I feel a little silly. See, sometimes my mom tells this story to other people, and I hate that. I wish she wouldn't tell stories about me. It's embarrassing! So I've decided to tell the story myself and take control of the situation!

One day, Mom came back from shopping, and I knew she had something special. I could tell by the way she was talking to us dogs. We watched carefully as she emptied the shopping bags. I was trying really hard to be patient, but sometimes it's hard to wait so long!

Finally, I saw it: a pack of three, huge, stuffed dragon toys! There are three dogs in our house, so it was meant to be!

We raced around expectantly while Mom got some scissors to remove the packaging, and then she handed each of us a new toy. Raika got the green dragon, Lyra got the blue one, and I got the purple one! I loved mine! All of us held our new toys with wagging tails and happy faces. I was so happy; this was like the best day of my life!

But then something happened. Raika's dragon squeaked.

I didn't know that Raika's dragon squeaked. I stopped chewing and dropped my dragon. Raika, of course, was extra happy because she got the best one, the one that squeaks! Raika knew that I was sad, but she didn't even care. Sometimes, I think she likes it when I'm sad, so that made me even more upset!

My new toy sat at my feet, abandoned. I was so sad and so mad all at the same time! I didn't want Raika to have the best dragon; I wanted to have it for myself!

Mom kept encouraging me to pick up my dragon, but I didn't want that boring toy. I knew I should be grateful for my new toy, but I wasn't. I wanted the squeaking one! Then Mom walked over to Lyra's toy and squeezed it for her. It squeaked too, just like

Raika's toy! Lyra happily claimed her dragon and carried it away.

And there I stood, miserable. I couldn't help it; I was so unhappy standing next to a stupid, silent, stuffed dragon while I watched my sisters with their squeaking ones. Even Lyra didn't care about me! How could I be happy when my sisters had extra special toys and mine was just ordinary? I mean, it can be hard to love my sisters when they get things that I don't have.

I knew that Mom was trying to tell me something in human language, but I was too sad to hear her at first. But then I could tell by her pointing and her words that she wanted me to pick up the toy. Finally she picked up my dragon, squeezed it, and... it squeaked!

My dragon squeaked, too! I was so excited that I grabbed my toy back! I loved my new dragon! I wagged my tail and chewed and squeaked with a big happy face, and all of my jealousy was gone. I was not sad or mad at anyone now. How could I be? I had a squeaking dragon, and it was purple— my favorite color!

So that's my jealousy story. I still get jealous sometimes, but that one was extra embarrassing because it was a misunderstanding. The funny thing is I don't even think about those toys anymore. I wonder where they are?

I have lots of toys around the house that I can play with, but my favorite games don't even use toys all that much. My favorite games are the ones my mom and I play together. Comment and let me know if you'd like to hear about them. Maybe you can teach them to your family!

COMMENTS:

Bruno (Lab) | Naples, FL, USA
I had so many toys around the house that my mom would trip on them at night! Now I have to clean them up before bedtime. Don't feel bad about being jealous. We all get jealous sometimes. I definitely want to hear about games that you play with your mom!

Amy (Golden Retriever) | Troy, NY, USA
Where did your mom get the dragons? I love dragons, and we have three dogs here too!

Lexi (German Shepherd) | Stowe, VT, USA
I don't have any dog toys. I wish I did.

Brito: Hey Lexi, Brito here! Start chewing on the side of the house or the patio furniture. That's an easy way to get someone to buy you a few toys of your own.

Sally (Border Collie) | Bar Harbor, ME, USA
You were jealous over a squeaky toy? That's stupid.

Champ: How would you feel if your mom stopped playing with you and started playing with a different dog instead? You would be jealous too!

Sally: That's different! People are not toys!

Champ: That's just your opinion. It's okay if you don't like toys. It's also okay if Brito does like toys! We can all be different. No need to judge! And Brito? I want to hear more about those games you play with your mom!

Brito: Coming right up!

8

Bath!

Posted by CaBrito

Today I was going to write about the games that mom and I play, but then I was horribly mistreated! Let me tell you what happened...

The day started out fine. I had a tasty breakfast, a fast-paced play session, and a nap in the sun. Mom sat down at her computer, and I hopped on her lap for a nap like I always do. Sounds perfect, right?

And then I heard her sniffing the air. That's weird; Mom doesn't usually sniff that much. Seriously, I didn't think she could smell things at all!

Next thing I knew, she grabbed me tight and stood up. What's up with that? I don't like to be picked up, and she knows that! I struggled, but she didn't let me go.

Mom got a towel and soap and placed them on the kitchen table. Next, she started the water running in the sink— this was terrible! Last time she put me in water, she took away all of that amazing "Eau d'Brito" that I had spent months collecting on my outdoor adventures!

Plop. Into the sink. Scrub-a-dub Brito.

Can I tell you a secret? The scrubbing part is okay. I kinda like the way mom scratches the soap all over my body, but I try not to let her know. What I don't like is the way she's making me smell disgusting, like flowers and soap!

So one moment, I'm totally enjoying that full body scratch, and the next, I'm scrabbling to escape. I almost made it! I climbed halfway onto the counter before she grabbed my collar and plopped me back into the sink.

There was no hope. The bath would continue.

Five minutes later, she was almost done. I was mortified; I smelled like a Poodle. But then, as she adjusted the water, she took her hands off me, and I saw my chance!

I leapt onto the counter and then onto a chair— I was free!

So I did what every dog has ever done since time began: I ran!!!

I raced through the house and skidded on the floors as I went around the corners. Bam! Into a wall! My feet were wet, and I was soapy; my traction was terrible. I got my feet back under me, and off I went. Bam! Into another wall! I didn't care. I would not be caught.

And you know what? In spite of the fact that I kept skidding into walls around corners, it was really pretty fun.

I shook, and soap and water splashed everywhere! I got some speed up, and under the table I went. I ran off to the family room and… the back door was open! Woot! I escaped into the backyard and rolled in the dirt and the leaves.

Once I made my exit into the great outdoors, mom gave up. She headed back into the house, shut the door, and left me to regain my delicious terrier smell.

I wasn't mad anymore; mostly I was tired. I still smelled a lot like Poodle, but at least I had fun. Then I realized that it was almost dinnertime and I was hungry, so I headed back inside.

Mom scooped me up and plopped me back in the

sink! Except this time, I was too tired to care. She rinsed the rest of the soap out of my hair, toweled me off, put me back on the floor, and guess what?! I got my second wind! I did a repeat performance— minus the soap splatters on the wall— but mom got smart and shut the door, foiling my grand finale.

A bit later she brought me dinner, and now I'm going to settle in for a nap. I'll probably have nightmares over the bath, but the rest... the rest was fun.

Comments:

Bruno (Lab) | Naples, FL, USA
Sorry you had to endure that, Brito. I've had baths too, but I've never escaped! You've given me hope; next time I will try harder to break free.

Sally (Border Collie) | Bar Harbor, ME, USA
Your mom washed you in the sink? I don't fit in the sink, so I get washed in a big tub outside. Sometimes I shake really hard, and soap and water fly everywhere! That part is the best because everyone squeals and runs away! After I have a bath, I'm very pretty and fluffy!

Champ: Sally, I'd love to see what you look like after a bath!

Sally: Don't hold your breath, Champ.

Keegan (Collie) | Dartmouth, NS, CAN

I know that the bath was traumatic, but don't forget to tell us about the games that you play with your mom. We're waiting!

9
Games We Play
Posted by CaBrito

I'm pretty much over the bath incident and back to my normal good smelling Terrier Self. Since you guys said you want to hear about games, I'm going to teach you a few of the ones I like to play with Mom. I love games! Mom and I play lots of silly games. Here are some of my favorites:

Chase the Ball

In this game, Mom sits on the floor and throws my soft, squishy ball across the room. I run and find it and pounce on it! I like to pretend that I am a big, wild wolf pouncing on my dinner, but I know I'm not really a wolf. Then I bring my ball back so that Mom can throw it again!

Sometimes I get tired of playing Chase the Ball, so I just sit down and chew on it. Then Mom sits on the floor with me and waits till I want to play again. Other times, Mom runs out of the room and hides. Then she calls me, and I have to find her; then we're playing Hide and Seek! Usually, I bring my ball with me.

After we sit for a while, she gives me a treat, so I put my ball down to eat my treat. I like my treat so much that I forget I was chewing on the ball! Then I will look up with my happy smiling face and wait for her to throw my ball again. This is one of my favorite games!

Chase the Treats!

Here's another great game. It's probably the best game ever!

Mom starts the game with a handful of dog treats for me. She throws a treat, and I run and eat it! Just as I swallow, she says my name and throws another treat in a new direction! I run and eat that one too! And then she does it again! I learned this game the very first day I moved in because it was so easy to learn. I always look at her right away when she says my name so that I can see where she is going to throw the next treat.

Sometimes, I don't see where the treat goes, so I have to use my nose to find it. That's okay— in fact, that's a great game too! What dog doesn't like a game of Find the Lost Treat?

Chase the Mommy!

Wait till you hear about this game. Remember how we play Chase the Ball and Chase the Treat? Well in this game, I chase my mommy!

To start the game, she says my name. When I look at her, she runs away as fast as she can! If she is very fast, then she will hide before I can even start playing. Then we're back to Hide and Seek!

When I find Mom, she sits on the floor and claps and talks in her squeaky voice and sometimes gives me an extra treat. I love it! We have played this

game so much that she never gets to hide anymore because I'm too fast!

But I don't get tired of the game! I still love to chase her in the house and then jump on her when she sits on the floor.

Scratch My Belly

If you think that I roll over and Mom scratches my belly in this game, then you would be right! I roll over on my back when my tummy is itchy, and then she scratches me all the way from the top of my chest down to my bellybutton! Because this game makes me feel sleepy and warm and tired, it is often the last game that we play before I take a nap.

We still play even though I am grown up now. Play time is the best time of the day! We run, we tumble, we chase, and I eat treats and play with toys! But we never play any game for very long; I always wish it was more!

I love my mommy better than anyone in the whole world. I try very hard to listen to her human words because I like to make her happy.

Speaking of listening, I go to school to learn some human words. I like going to school! Sometimes my human siblings complain about going to school, but not me. I think school is really fun! At school, my mom teaches me things that I want to learn; and anyway, school time feels a lot like morning play time, except I have to listen more carefully to the human words. What's not to like?

One thing I learned at doggy school was how to come when the humans call my name. That was easy to do when I wasn't doing anything else, but a lot harder when I had something even more interesting to do. Mom was patient, and now I try hard to cooperate, even when I'd rather dig a hole or run around outside.

I also learned how to stay in one place. Boy was that hard. It took a lot of time to learn because I don't like to sit still! Heck, who likes to sit still? Even my human brothers barely sit still, and they are a lot older than I am!

Do you want to know how Mom taught me to come to my name and to stay in one spot? I'll tell you in my next blog, so stay tuned!

COMMENTS:

Bruno (Lab) | Naples, FL, USA
OMG, we play the treat chasing game and the belly rub game too!

Theo (Great Dane) | Palo Alto, CA, USA
Your mom plays the Best. Games. Ever!

Champ (Terrier) | Portsmouth, NH, USA
Have you ever lost a treat under the couch and couldn't get it back? I lost a treat under the couch months ago, and I still think about it. I'm waiting for Mom to move the couch.

Brito: Champ, you read my mind! That totally happened to me recently, and I'm going to write a story about it in a few weeks. Don't forget to subscribe so you can read it!

Sally (Border Collie) I Bar Harbor, ME, USA

There is more to life than play. When are you going to start working and being responsible?

Champ: There is also more to life than work. When you are going to start to play? Why don't you come over for a playdate so I can teach you?

Sally: Never!

10

Going to School

Posted by CaBrito

I love going to dog school! I learn all kinds of things there, like how to come when someone calls my name or how to stay still. Do you want to know how my mom taught these things to me? I hope so, because that's what I'm going to tell you today.

Here's how I learned to come when Mom calls my name. Mom would say my name, and when I looked at her, she would sit on the floor and encourage me to come over for a visit. There was nothing else to do, so I would come to her. After a nice pat and scratch, she would reach into her pocket and give me a treat. Wow! That was pretty cool!

All day long, Mom would call my name, and every time, the same thing happened— she would sit on the floor, scratch me, and give me another treat! Sometimes she didn't have a treat with her, so we would go to the treat jar together and get one. But that was okay; I didn't mind the short wait.

After a few days, I would come running when I heard my name! It was hard when there were other things that I wanted to do, but mostly Mom called me when I wasn't doing anything, so I got into a pretty good habit of listening. After a while, Mom started to call me when I was doing interesting things. After I came, she would give me a treat and then send me back to whatever I was doing. Wow!! Win-win! I got to keep playing my own games, plus I scored a bonus treat!

And the best part? She never calls me when she's mad at me or to yell at me. Once she called me while I was carrying a dirty sock that I had found on the floor. Even though I wasn't supposed to have the sock, she gave me a treat for coming, and then put the sock in the laundry. So now when I find things on the floor that aren't supposed to be there, I bring them to her, even when I want to chew them up. Then I get treats and the house is kept cleaner to boot. Another win-win!

Now I'm so good at coming back when called that I don't even care if I get a treat. I know that when Mom calls me, I should come running because it's always good to see what she wants.

Sometimes when I forget to come when I'm called, Mom gives my treats to Raika instead. Like I said before, Raika has no sense of adventure, and she's always with Mom anyway. I hate it when Raika gets my treats, so now I'm even better about listening for my name.

But staying in one place? That was so hard to learn! What Mom did was get me my very own washcloth. I'm not very big, so I had a washcloth. But the big dogs— they get bath mats! I know it sounds weird, so let me tell you how the washcloth helped me learn to stay in one place.

Mom put the washcloth on the floor, and of course I was curious, so I went to see it. As soon as I sniffed it, she threw a treat on top of the washcloth. Of course I ate that treat and looked around for more! And guess what? She gave me more! My mom stood right there feeding me treats! Then I got distracted by something, and I walked away. When I looked back, my washcloth was gone. That was sad.

The next day I saw her drop my washcloth on the ground again. To be honest, I had forgotten about the treats the day before, but I was still curious, so I walked over to check out the washcloth. Guess what happened? If you said she dropped more treats on the towel, then you would be right! As soon as I got there, more treats showed up! And the best part was that, as long as I stood on that washcloth, she fed me treats.

Soon I learned to run over to wait on the towel and eat! After a while Mom didn't give me as many treats, but I was still happy on my towel.

Sometimes I would get bored and leave, but she didn't seem to mind. She would just pick up the washcloth and I would have to wait until it came back to try again.

Soon, I wouldn't leave that washcloth for anything, even when she rang the doorbell! The washcloth game is really great! All of us dogs play it at the same time, and Mom can't fool us into leaving no matter what she does!

Now that I'm good at those things, I'm learning a lot of fancy tricks, like how to pick things up off the floor and how to leap in the air and jump over jumps! Sometimes Mom has me show my tricks to other people, but that's a story for another day.

COMMENTS:

Amy (Golden Retriever) | Troy, NY, USA
Wow! I've never heard of the washcloth game. That sounds like a great way to learn to stay put!

Sally (Border Collie) | Bar Harbor, ME, USA
Brito, I'd love to learn more about your advanced tricks some day. I know a few myself. Maybe our moms could trade ideas.

11

Stuck Ball

Posted by CaBrito

One day, while Mom and I were playing the chase the ball game with my squishy ball, Mom threw my ball under the cabinet. I tried to get it back, but I couldn't reach. I barked a few times to call for help.

I wasn't really worried; this happens pretty often. I saw Mom sweep her hands under the cabinet. I wagged my tail to encourage her, and.... nothing came out! Well, that's not quite true. A bunch of paper and garbage came out, but not my ball!

Mom usually takes care of this sort of problem lickety split, so I wagged my tail at her to let her know I still believed in her. I waited there as she went off to get a stick. Swoop under the cabinet with the stick! I waited! And... nothing came out!

That's okay. I'm an optimist. I looked up at her with my still happy face and wagged my tail again. I was telling her, "Keep going, Mom! You can do it!"

This time she got a flashlight to look for my ball, but now her expression was very puzzled. That concerned me just a bit. I gave her a few more tentative tail wags to keep her in the hunt, but when she started looking in other areas, my concern grew. I knew it was under that cabinet. Dogs have very good noses so we know things like that.

Then she got a new stick! This time she went from the top down to get my ball, rather than from underneath. I hadn't seen that before, but I wasn't worried because sometimes she knows about things that I haven't learned yet.

Go, Mom, go!!

Next thing I knew, she left the room for a minute and came back. She reached under the cabinet, and... pulled the ball out from underneath! I pounced!!

Wait. That was NOT the ball I lost under the cabinet. That was a different ball. I rejected the impostor and went back to the cabinet to show her that I was not fooled. Not cool, Mom. Not cool at all.

My confidence was starting to waver, but I reminded myself that we all make mistakes. Admittedly, trying to fool me with a different ball wasn't a nice thing to do, but I could pretend that didn't happen. I'm good like that.

Next, Mom left the room and came back with my stuffed frog. I do love my stuffed frog, but right then I did not want a stuffed frog. I wanted my ball. The one under the cabinet. I wanted her to get that one for me. Please.

I tried to keep wagging my tail to encourage her, but let's face it: I was losing faith. It occurred to me I might have to keep vigil at the cabinet all night if she couldn't get it back, and that didn't look too cozy.

She got another stick. This time she attached duct tape to the top and tried to fish my ball out. No go—

it just brought out an awful lot of dust and dirt. Wow. I love my mom, but her housekeeping sure leaves something to be desired!

Next she threw my frog behind the cabinet at the ball. Why did she do that?! Maybe I didn't want my frog right then, but that doesn't mean I wanted it stuck behind the cabinet with all of the other random garbage that was coming out. Now my ball was stuck AND my frog was gone to boot.

I got tired of wagging my tail. I lay quietly a few feet away with my head on my paws. I was losing hope. This utter failure to take care of my most prized possessions had never happened before.

Mom went to consult with the other humans in the house. That was promising! Everyone trooped in and looked underneath the cabinet.

First, Chris reached underneath, but he came out empty handed. Out came the flashlight and the stick, and the whole family took turns looking underneath. More attempts to rescue my toys led to nothing. I was desolate. I thought I might have to live there forever mourning my stuck ball. I could do that, you know, but I didn't want to.

Next, Nick lay down on the ground and started

feeling around. He was trying really, really hard. The other humans were coaching him. Everyone was helping; my whole team was on board! They had the stick, the flashlight, and a lot of words!!

Go, team, go!!

I started wagging my tail again. My ears came up, and my eyes were bright. I looked over the top of the rescuer to see better, and… there it was! My bestest, oldest, most ratty squishy ball came out! And my frog too!   Dirty, but unharmed!

I grabbed my ball, zoomed around the bedroom, wagged my tail at everyone, kissed the boy rescuer, and settled down to nurse my ball back to health. Wagging all the time.

COMMENTS:

Champ (Terrier) | Portsmouth, NH, USA
I can't believe your mom tried the bait and switch trick on you! Does she think you're stupid?

 Brito: It hasn't happened since, so I think she learned not to do that.

Bruno (Lab) | Naples, FL, USA
Wow, another nail biter of a story! I'm glad that your family was there to help rescue your special ball.

Keegan (Collie) | Dartmouth, NS, CAN
Great story, Brito! I have lost things under the furniture myself, and my mom always gets it back for me.

Lexi (German Shepherd)| Stowe, VT, USA

Brito, I have great news! My family brought me in the house and gave me toys! I tried your trick about howling all night and chewing on the patio furniture, and it really worked! And guess what? I think they like having me in the house! And I am very happy to be here! Thanks so much for your help.

Brito: Lexi, that is so wonderful! This might be a good time to start teaching them your body language. A good one is to place your chin on their laps when you want something, like a pet or a treat off their plate. But try not to drool. Let us know how it goes!

Stella (Lab) | Ottawa, ON, CAN

Since Lexi shared her good news, I want to share my good news, too! My mom read your blog, and my family gave me a special area to call my own— no kids allowed! Thanks so much for helping my family be an even better home for me!

Brito: Stella, I'm so happy for you! I think every dog should have a special place where they can go and no kids are allowed to follow.

 **Sally** (Border Collie) | Bar Harbor, ME, USA
I still think you spend too much energy on play and not enough on work.

 Champ: Sally, how about that playdate? I can teach you how to dig in my dog sandbox!

 Sally: Maybe. I'll ask my mom.

12

Vacation!

Posted by CaBrito

My family is going on vacation! Yep, that's right—and it's my first one! I'm so excited that I've already put my toys in a pile by the door so no one will forget them. Even Raika is excited; she was so happy, she played chase with me! After a minute she remembered that she doesn't play, but hey, it's a start! Maybe I just need to be more patient with her. Anyway, I wanted to let you guys know that I would be gone for a while so you won't worry about me.

I love my blog! And I love all of you, my new friends! As soon as I get back, I'll tell you about where I went and what we did. But in the meantime, don't forget to subscribe! Talk later!

COMMENTS:

Bruno (Lab) I Naples, FL, USA
Have a great time! Don't forget to bring spare balls because sometimes they get lost in the woods.

Brito: Good advice, Bruno! Thanks!

Sally (Border Collie) I Bar Harbor, ME, USA
Make sure you bring a hairbrush so that your family can brush you at night. Otherwise, you might have to sleep on stickers in your hair. Have fun, Brito!

Champ: Fun? Did Sally just use the "fun" word? Rock on, Sally!

Sally: I wasn't talking to you, Champ. I was talking to Brito.

Brito: Hey guys, this isn't the time to argue! I'm heading out on an adventure! Woot!!

Champ: Good point, Brito. Sally, I was just kidding.

 Sally: Apology accepted, Champ. Mom said I could come over to dig in your sandbox, so I'll see you tomorrow.

Made in the USA
Middletown, DE
30 July 2019